The Eastern F
A World War II
Novel
RICHARD G. HOLE

The Eastern Front
A World War II Novel

Richard G. Hole

World War II

SYNOPSIS

The Russians were advancing on all fronts ...

Millions of German soldiers did not understand that those ragged and dirty Russian soldiers, who had pushed the vicinity of Moscow, to the other side of the Volga and to the oil regions of Baku; those men who fled or fell prisoners by the millions, in a concept of mass that no European could conceive, were now launching themselves on the German troops and those of their allies, with an unprecedented power.

The world shook to the beat of the fighting on the Eastern front.

Millions of beings were there engaged in the most colossal battle in history.

German soldiers, hungry, poorly dressed, exposed to freezing, malnourished and low on ammunition, clung to the ground in the hope of preventing the enemy from setting foot on Germany.

The Eastern Front is a story belonging to the World War II collection, a series of war novels developed in World War II.

RICHARD G. HOLE

THE EASTERN FRONT

FOREWORD

A little further north of the recently conquered Viadsma, Captain Trauber's Company was slowly making its way to the small town of Tepluja.

Throughout that night, false by the incessant light of the flares and the purple lightning of the shots, the men continued to hit their positions on the snow soiled by the rain that had followed, destroyed by the fatigue of the operations carried out. out and eager to pause, a bit, to be able, at least, to verify that they existed.

Because, in reality, since they emerged from a flaming Viadsma, with the lonely streets crossed by electrical wires, full of the most heteroclite objects and reeking of the stench of dead horses, their horizon had become a line, which, starting from from their eyes, it crossed the sights of their weapons and ended down there, in the confused panorama in which the silhouettes of the Russian soldiers moved, like fast shadows.

Outside of that line of fire, nothing, not even the body itself, had manifested itself in a way to believe in its existence. The muscles stiff from the cold and the organism numb from hunger and fatigue, the only thing that lived palpably in them was the desire to move forward that was concentrated in the gaze towards the point of view.

Behind them the artillery raised a constant thunderclap and animated the air above their hulls in a coming and going of hisses that hooted like swift invisible birds until they became lightning bolts over enemy lines.

The Russians, having created a withdrawal vacuum behind them, were now offering insistent resistance, as German weapons approached Moscow. The speed that until then had allowed a mechanical war, in which the armored vehicles played the best trick, became with the arrival of the snow, in a raw fight of men who suffered and died to advance a single step on the hard earth.

Close to the ground like his men, Karl Trauber, surrounded by some non-commissioned officers who served as Staff, anxiously awaited the arrival of dawn to finally jump over the shattered hovels that could be glimpsed in the pale light of the explosions.

Aware of the state of his boys, the captain wanted to give them a break, however brief, to see again on their dirty and bearded faces, the smile in which every leader clearly reads a spirit of victory.

The earth seemed to boil in a formidable boil that reached his entrails in a series of convulsions, as if the poor earth were seriously ill, manifesting its pain in those shudders that passed directly to the bodies of the men who were desperately embraced by it.

"Trauber Company?

"Yes sir.

"Get me the captain.

"Right away.

"Tell me?

"This is Commander Strauffer. How's that going, Karl?

"As always, sir. We are still waiting for dawn to start the assault.

"Any idea of the enemy forces in front of you?

"None, my commander.

"It's okay. However, be very careful when entering Tepluja. It seems that the men of Semurow are camping in these surroundings.

"The partisan?

"Yes. Be very careful, Trauber. Let no boy be separated from his unit. He will remember how heroes end up in the hands of that bandit

"I'll keep that in mind, sir. Does the same time follow for the initiation of the artillery fire?

"Exactly at six fifty-two. At seven o'clock, we will take the shot to the road and the bridge behind the town. It will be time to jump in, Trauber.

"Anything else, my commander?

"Nothing, boy. "Good chance!", As the English say.

"Thank you very much, my commander. At your service.

As always, in the last hours of the night, silence had spread over the front like an omen that heralded the storm that would break out in a few hours. But the calm of the small universe that surrounded them was fraught with danger, since everyone knew that those tremendous hours of waiting were often used for strokes.

... "It seems that the men of Semurow are camping in these surroundings. Be very careful, Trauber. You will remember how heroes end up in the hands of that bandit ..."

Strauffer's words kept ringing obsessively in Karl's ears. Those words had made him shudder, much to his regret, because they contained a recent experience, a thousand kilometers behind, near the Polish border, in a forest whose only memory was capable of making the hair of any man in the Company stand on end. he could be counted, miraculously, as a survivor.

SEMUROW!

Some kind of tiger disguised as a man. That was what the general had called him when he reported that terrible attack in which the men who dared to separate from his Unit ... appeared the next day hanging in bunches from the trees of the forest.

The impossible had been done to capture that species of beast that left in its wake a trail of death and desolation as never before had the Armed Unit bequeathed it ... But all the efforts were in vain; Semurow resolved itself in the air like that dirty mist that preceded Russian dawns.

Trauber was obliged to let his men know that Semurow was prowling around. But, deep in his heart, the captain felt a great duty to communicate this bad news. And, it was not because of a lack of confidence in the boys, but because, tired as they were and ready to launch themselves, at dawn, against the enemy positions, the news would not stop disturbing the veterans and worrying, perhaps excessively. , to those who had not seen their companions hanging from the trees.

"- Otto!

The bond rushed to the side of his superior.

"My captain?

"Inform all officers that the Battalion has learned that Semurow is around. Let the Section commanders bring it to their females. The slogan is this: No man for any reason should abandon his contact with the Unit to which he belongs. That the Platoon leaders do not lose sight of their boys during the assault. Understood?

"Yes sir.

The news was already released!

Karl tried to imagine what would go through the minds of each of his men. He was perfectly sure that the veterans would grit their teeth, hoping for the chance to see Semurow on the other side of their sharp bayonets. As for the "newbies" ... Who would be able to delve into the thoughts of men who do not know each other?

Slowly, the shadows of the night were disintegrating; as if blackness were a living body voraciously eaten by the moth of light. The outlines of things became clear, at first blurred, then the details emerged from the darkness that had been hidden from them until then.

Five kilometers behind the Company, the silence was torn by artillery fire. Clouds of projectiles, in dense flocks, began to cross the space to open in the town their livid fans of death ...

With his eyes fixed on the luminous dial of his watch, Trauber followed the movement of the seconds hand in steps. Thus, the time that the artillery preparation lasted lasted a century for the captain. Finally, no longer able to control his nerves, he drew his signal pistol, firing the red attack light.

As the explosions of the artillery shells passed into the background, the fire from the infantry weapons filled the gray space between the two lines.

Karl, followed by the men who made up his Piana Mayor, quickly crossed the distance that separated him from the vanguard line, positioning himself behind the Third Section, which was the one that was progressing along the axis of the offensive.

One after another, protecting each other, the Platoons were closing the distance that separated them from the enemy. For the moment, it was the automatic weapons that had the floor. However, from time to time, the dry explosion of a mortar tore apart the monotony of the machine-gun fire.

The Germans, while advancing, kept within a total connection, continuing to carry out a crossfire plan, each time a small Unit stood out in the vanguard. Thus, in stages, they arrived near the first houses that had continued to burn since they had been bombarded by German cannons.

Until that moment, everything had been reduced to a close combat between the fantastic maze of enemy projectiles that wove invisible networks of death. Now the real fight began, the main program of which was to dislodge the enemy from every resistance post that he had set out to maintain.

The Third Section launched its first Battalion against the nearest house. Sticking to the ground, the men began to slide, elbows, into the burning ruins in front of them. Meanwhile, the machine guns covered them with a dense fire that raised, when they collided with the burning beams, a very rapid constellation of sparks.

After having two of his men advance on the flanks, to prevent the enemy from retreating without casualties, Sergeant Kopler began the assault on the house, previously throwing some grenades through the illuminated holes that the Artillery had opened.

The crumbling building seemed to be brutally startled, and some of its already half-collapsed walls fell in formidable dust. Kopler and his boys did not wait any longer. With bayonets drawn, submachine gun in hand, or an unsecured grenade, they brutally stormed into the ruins, opening fire to the right and left.

But, as they already thought, despite everything, they found within the adequate answer to their "insinuations". The Russians, hiding in the strongest part of the house, launched themselves like wolves against the assailants.

And, as always, above the powerful and modern weapons that armies boast of, victory had to be won by the element, by the decisive factor in war: Man.

The melee began inside the house, under the bloody light of the fire. One of the German soldiers paid with his life for the definitive victory of his own. Seconds later, the three Russians occupying the ruins had ceased to exist.

Having overcome the initial resistance, Trauber ordered the general advance, spreading the fight, house by house, throughout the town. The streets appeared completely deserted before the Germans and in the shadow of each building there seemed to be trap, betrayal and hatred, hand in hand with death.

Two hours and twelve men cost the Company absolute control of the town. Slowly, trudging, shattered with exhaustion, their faces and hands blackened by gunpowder smoke and their uniforms torn apart, the Germans gathered in the center of what little was left of Tepluja. The First Section, which had not suffered any casualties, was in charge of setting up a provisional defense line on the northern edge of the town. The rest, by order of Karl, formed among the ruins.

It was then, during the count, that everyone realized that a platoon from the Fourth had disappeared with their sergeant ...

There was no need for anyone to open their mouths to attempt an explanation. In everyone's mind, like a brutal flash of lightning to clarify ideas, a single word had just appeared.

SEMUROW!

Trauber clenched his fists. He was sure that inside the town he would not find the slightest trace of his men. Thus, after ordering the three Sections to take a well-deserved rest and prepare a hot ranch, he headed, followed by his Deputy Sergeant Kramer, to the front line.

Long before arriving, he was already approached by a link running to meet him.

"Captain!

"What happen?

The man lowered his eyes. The emotion was clear on his face.

"They are there in front! Was the laconic reply.

Karl didn't ask him more. So that? He kept walking until he reached the place where the Section had been installed. His boss, Lieutenant Lukas, came looking for him.

But Trauber didn't even look at him. His eyes, above the officer's shoulders, were fixed on the macabre scene that served as the horizon for the First ...

Alió below, less than a hundred meters from the new line of fire, stood out against the monotony of the plain, two trees and an "isba". This one could not attract anyone's attention, as it was nothing more than a pile of dried manure. The trees ...

There were the men of the missing Squad. They hung from the branches like ghoulish fruits that human wickedness had brought forth from the bare arms of the tree. It was not necessary to count them; Even from their appearance, despite their distance, Trauber was able to recognize them, nevertheless, the terrible similarity that the horrendous death had given them.

That scene bore a signature, unmistakable, indubitable; as true as if the author were there, shouting his name: SEMUROW!

Lukas gazed, with his twins, at the macabre place.

"I have not dared to go for them, to bury them, because I am sure that there is someone in the" isba ".

In turn, Karl focused his binoculars on the squalid construction. Insistently, on the circular horizon of the optics, he toured every detail of the "isba". Everything seemed quiet, abandoned, definitely dead like the men who hung from the trees. The proximity of those executed gave the "isba" an intimate sense of tragedy

However...

Trouber reached without knowing exactly why, with the same conclusion as the head of the First Section. Something intimate, which came to him as a warning from his unconscious, warned him against that ridiculous hovel, so apparently quiet.

At the idea that Semurow was inside, his teeth gritted loudly as his jaws clenched. Then, without ceasing to observe the 'isba' and, therefore, without turning around.

"Leave me four men, Lukas!

The lieutenant looked at his superior in amazement. He had understood his words perfectly, and yet he could not believe what he had just heard.

"But, sir ..." he dared to protest.

"I have ordered you, Lieutenant Lukas, to prepare four men. I will go with them to see what happens in that "isba". I don't think Semurow is waiting for us there; but, if it were, I wouldn't miss this occasion for the world ... "he paused as he put the cufflinks in their sheath." Besides, you have to pick up those guys.

Lukas didn't dare to say anything more. Minutes later, he returned to the captain with the four requested men.

Trauber shot the soldiers a sympathetic look. Then darkening the face again.

"Go! He ordered starting to advance.

As he crossed the front line, which was nothing more than a group of holes made by shovel force an hour earlier, Karl gestured for the men following him to bow their bodies. Then, doing the same, he began to run, zigzag, towards the "isba".

The entire First Section was on the guns. The men were ready to defend, in whatever way, the life of their captain. Any of them would have sincerely wished they were in Karl's place so as not to suffer from that awful nervous tension. From the beginning of the war, on the plains of Poland, in the blitzkrieg of the West, Trauber's men had learned a great deal about this captain; enough to love him with a wonderful intensity and camaraderie.

Trauber advanced without taking his eyes off the silent "isba." He did not wish for their speedy destruction, which he would have achieved by sending the Flamethrower Squad, because, like a strange and paradoxical intuition, he was certain that someone was inside.

A wounded soldier or someone who had failed to escape at the right time. The idea that Semurow himself was there, badly injured, could not get out of his mind.

At his gesture, two of the men who were marching, like him, hunched over and ready to fight, swiftly passed to the invisible side of the "isba". In no way did Trauber want his prey to escape at the last moment.

Then, giving one more proof of his recklessness and when no one expected him to do so, he burst into the interior of the hut, before his soldiers could prevent him.

Light filtered inside through a small hole at one end of the concave thatched roof. Karl, trigger ready, took a quick look inside.

What he saw was in no way a danger to anyone.

Backing away, he stuck out his left arm, gesturing for his men to enter. Then he advanced again towards the two human figures that were in the corner of the hut.

From the moment he had entered the "isba" the girl's sobs had given him a clear idea of what had happened there. It must be the wife or sister of the man lying next to her.

Once the sunny ones were inside, the captain approached the Russian.

"Get up!

She turned her face, streaked with the tears that used to flow abundantly from her blue eyes. Two blonde braids, tied with two dirty bows, divided a beautiful, silky head of hair.

He got up awkwardly, still taking his eyes off the man on the ground. Karl, in turn, leaned over and with the flashlight, since that corner was almost completely dark, illuminated the Russian's face.

Was dead. A hole in the forehead indicated where the bullet had entered. This man was old and dressed like the peasants, not being, therefore, no combatant element of the Soviet forces.

"Who is this man? He inquired turning to the Russian.

She stared into the German's eyes. The latter, through the tears that continued to flow gently, falling on the girl's face, believed he read a pain that could not be explained with any word.

"Nitchevo! She replied.

"You don't understand German? Trauber asked again, expressing himself in what little Russian he knew.

"Nitchevo! "The girl answered again.

Karl began to understand that the nervous "shock" must have altered the Russian's faculties. Because, to every question that was asked, she invariably answered with the most negative word in her language.

"Take her to the village," Trauber ordered. And, seeing that one of the soldiers stayed. "Wait for me outside! I am coming right away.

There was no reason to do what he was supposed to do. But, that rare intuition of the beginning, still weighed heavily on his soul. Once the soldier obeyed the order to leave, Trauber knelt next to the dead old man and nervously began to search him. After a few seconds, he found the man's threadbare and dirty wallet. Using the flashlight, he examined the documents and his eyes shone brightly, realizing that his intuition had not deceived him.

Hastily tucking the wallet into one of his pockets, he continued to search the body, finding nothing but a chain hanging from his neck. Delicately, he unzipped it, putting it away with the documents as well.

Once outside, he went to the soldier who was waiting for him.

"Give me your rifle and carry the corpse of that man. We are going to bury him in the village cemetery.

* * *

A week, short like all pleasant things in which time seems to go faster, cruelly shortening the pleasure, passed and flew. The orders had already arrived to continue the advance and the men, with sullen faces, began the preparations, cursing that this wonderful rest would end so soon.

But there was not all the joy of Tepluja in the rest, the hot ranch, the quiet guards and the games of cards that had provided them with a joyous well-being.

There was also "Miss Nitchevo".

That's what they all called her, since no one had managed to make her say another word.

Since the old Russian was buried, with a certain solemnity, in the village cemetery, in front of her, the young woman, without saying another word than the only one she seemed to know, had acted in a way that a man of the Company did not speak. did not feel an extraordinary affection for that creature.

Without saying a single word, but with a charming smile that fully illuminated her face, in which, generally, sadness reigned, "Miss Nitchevo" began to become the sister of all the men of the Company.

The scratches on the used uniforms began to disappear as if by magic, while, by a similar procedure, the buttons were in place, which they had long since abandoned, as well as the ugly pieces of wire that held the few that remained. .

Day and night, tireless at all hours, "Nitchevo" washed, sewed, arranged a thousand different things, still finding time to take a technical look at the kitchen where his silent advice was listened to with unusual attention.

Trauber's soldiers showered her with gifts. All the objects that had been bought with the intention of taking the road to the distant homeland, were delivered, with a simply emotional simplicity and sincerity to "Nitchevo", the sister of the Company.

Captain Trauber's two uniforms shone with a cleanliness no soldier had ever known. And the young woman, in the rare moments of rest that she allowed herself, went to visit the captain, sitting next to him and spending long periods of time contemplating him.

Karl had no doubt that the emotion of having witnessed the old man's death had caused the girl to be speechless, and she could not say more than the word that had served to baptize her.

Unfortunately, the hour of the march sounded and the Company prepared to continue towards the icy road that led to Moscow.

Trauber had obtained a special document, an "ausweis" signed by the general of the Sector so that nobody, in any case, would bother "Nitchevo". In addition, he managed to house her in the best house in Tepluja, recommending her care to the occupying forces that took over the town.

Later, at the time of the march and when the young woman was crying with the same intensity of that day of the "isba", Karl stroked her hair.

"We will be back soon," Nitchevo ", don't worry, take care of yourself ... and" he remembered the chain that he had taken from the old man and drying it, he handed it to the girl. " Take this, it belongs to you.

She raised her eyes to him, looking at him with an intensity he had never used before. Then, standing on tiptoe, she offered her fresh lips, in a simple and moving gesture in which all her wishes were summed up ...

CHAPTER ONE

"IVAN" REACTS

Luck changed course ...

During all those years of suffering, of pain, in which the soldiers were left on the snow like human landmarks, like traces of a historical past full of glory, luck had changed course.

It seemed as if cruel Fate was pleased to destroy the hopes of the West, giving victory to those who centuries before, mounted on small Tatar horses, endangered Europe and its Civilization.

The Russians were advancing on all fronts ...

For men like Trauber, events went beyond the area of their individual conception. And, like him, millions of German soldiers, did not manage to understand that those ragged and dirty soldiers, who had pushed the vicinity of Moscow, to the other side of the Volga and to the oil regions of Baku; those men who fled or fell prisoners by the millions, in a concept of mass that no European could conceive, were now launching themselves on the German troops and those of their allies, with an unprecedented power.

Everything that had cost so much blood to conquer, step by step, "isba" by "isba", leaving in each combat a growing number of lives, in that Russian land, with the whiteness of a shroud, in which the German graves were blacked out. , he was now abandoned in the flames of a technique that had belonged exclusively to the enemy.

The scorched earth!

Never more logically could this gathering of formidable fires that marked the places recently abandoned by the German army be called "lines of fire" now. A total war, tremendous as a posthumous act of something colossal that was already preparing for death.

What was left of the Trauber Company?

Very little thing! Across the length and breadth of that immense Soviet world, Karl's men lay beneath the cold surface of the earth, his last dream in a distant country, unlike anything they had ever known, strange and tremendous as its dimensions ...

The word "descent" seemed to have been permanently erased from the war dictionary of that time. Always backwards! Returning to see the same towns, the same cities that, years before, had been occupied and conquered with a smile on their lips.

The world shook to the beat of the fighting on the Eastern front. Millions of beings were there engaged in the most colossal battle in history. Hungry, poorly dressed, exposed to freezing, malnourished and low on ammunition, they clung to the ground in the hope of preventing the enemy from setting foot on Germany.

For Trauber, the constant defeat that the Russians inflicted on German weapons was, as for all combatants, the treacherous dagger of a disaster that, after the cyclopean efforts made, they were sure not to deserve.

The passage through Tepluja had, for all the boys, a special tone of sadness. The memories were still alive in their souls and their eyes searched anxiously, among the blackened ruins of the houses, the comforting image of "Nitchevo".

What would have become of her?

No one was there to answer the questions that burned the lips of those soldiers. The loneliness that precedes death, haunted the dirty streets of Tepluja, like a hateful ghost that repeated itself, a thousand times, every time they were about to leave a town.

During the few hours that they remained there, Karl, helplessly, walked the streets of Tepluja a hundred times in a row and a hundred times stopped in front of the ruins of the house where he had left "Nitchevo". Then, impelled by a superior force, he was in the cemetery, next to the old man's grave, on which some dried flowers remembered the girl's last visit.

TEPLUJA!

How soon all that happened! The enemy once again pushed furiously and Trauber, with the few men he had left, once again saw the bitterness, this time a little more intense, of seeing the mutilated remains of a town disappear on the horizon where, that could not be denied, he had sensed a happiness he had never enjoyed.

* * *

The Polish forests had succeeded or the Russian plains. For the sector in which Trauber's Company operated, the Soviet land, with its graves and generously watered with German blood, had disappeared forever. All that seemed a ground that was resting in the part of the mind where memories huddle, curling itself in the encystment of oblivion.

It was no longer just a question of refreshing the impetus of the Soviet army. Of trying to stop that gigantic avalanche of men that were thrown, like a tremendous avalanche, on the German positions.

The war was being lost ...

The General Staffs had only one obsession: to find footholds strong enough to be able, if not to stop, at least to divide the enemy's advance, thus subtracting power and penetration force.

This is what happened, for the Trauber Company, in that Polish outpost that received the name of THE FORTIN OF DESPERATION.

The order came to them as they were retreating through the south of the Warsaw region. A dusty motorcyclist, who had landed on the mud from the last rains and this one on the dust from the previous summer; in short, a dirty liaison agent like all those circulating on the immense front, stumbled upon the Company, after two days of having searched the entire Sector for it uselessly.

The document was signed by General Guderian's General Staff and had absolute priority over any other, since it emanated from the Higher Headquarters of the Army.

"From General Staff to Division 347.

(For his passage to the head of the Company, Karl Trauber.)

Absolute priority.

Very secret and important.

Upon immediate receipt of these instructions, you will proceed to occupy, without delay, the castle-fortress of Lotzzy. Once this operation has been carried out, he will take the part corresponding to his Superior Unit, with which he will definitely lose contact, since it will go to another Sector.

From the moment your Unit occupies Lotzzy's fortress-castle, you will be responsible to the homeland for its defense "a outrance". In no way and whatever the status, number and circumstance of your Unit, you will emerge from that Key position that must be defended "until death".

This General Staff expects the proven heroism of its Unit, the sacrifice necessary for the honorable defense of German territory.

General in Chief of the Armies
of the Third Reich.
(Unreadable.)

"Heil Hitler."

The strategic and tactical considerations of Lotzzy's fortress-castle were explained below. Surrounded for the most part by impassable swamps, it was the only point, for two hundred kilometers, through which the enemy could cross the line. If they did not go through that part, the Russians would have to travel a hundred kilometers through each part to enter the lower part of Poland.

The Lotzzy fort saved a considerable amount of troops that could be sent to other more precise presses.

Trauber launched his Unit and at dusk, always following the westerly direction, the sad and uninterrupted path of retreat.

The small garrison of auxiliary forces that occupied the fort, warmly received Trauber's Company. Too warmly for Trauber's opinion.

At that time, too many things were already beginning to be said that, months before, no one would have dared, not only to say, but almost to think. This was certainly the most painful thing for men like Karl whose head the painful idea of total defeat could not get into.

And it was, in fact, very difficult that after having formed part of the imposing hammer pylon that was the Army at the beginning of the campaign and in all those of Europe, that total collapse could be accepted as an irreparable thing.

There was in the hearts of many Germans, in those bitter hours, a hope as strong as the impulse that had carried them to all the battles of Europe with a smile of triumph on their lips. Every morning, every time the sky announced the presence of the less and less numerous friendly aviation, the good Germans looked up hopefully, hoping to see some of the wonderful "secret weapons" that Hitler had promised them.

For this reason, when Karl realized the insane joy with which he was received, as a relief, in that fort that had not yet suffered the ravages of war, the bitterness, when verifying the existence of cowardice, in a uniform in which He did not believe her capable, he felt a painful sensation of pain in his soul.

Preventing his men from talking to those who were leaving, he ordered their chief to leave the fort immediately. Then, when he found himself alone, in his room, with his thoughts, he preferred to dedicate himself to working intensely, to kill the memory of the painful words he had just heard.

The castle-fortress of Lotzzy was an old fortress that the Poles first and then the German engineers, had turned into a bastion strong enough to be defended with some ease.

On the east side, the fort materially sank into the river and on both sides, the north and the south, the swamps completely surrounded it, making it form a kind of peninsula, whose isthmus was formed by a narrow path that came out from the rear and pointing west.

In times of peace, the fort had a beautiful bridge that linked it to the east with the other side of the river, avoiding a detour of about one hundred and fifty kilometers. But, since the Germans invaded Poland, the bridge had been completely blown up, replaced by one of circumstances which, in turn, had been blown up days before Trauber's arrival at Lotzzy.

His Company had used pneumatic boats to cross the invisible line that joined both banks, since, to the right and left, a hundred meters downstream and upriver, the waters mixed with the quicksand of the swamp, making paths impassable. zones with any means of navigation.

When the occupants of the fort moved away, the vast area behind was completely deserted. The inhabitants of the two villages that could be seen from the ancient battlements had long ago fled, leaving the sad loneliness of abandonment in their wake. In this way, Trauber's Company was completely isolated, since, although it could leave through the back of the fort, the orders of the General Staff did not allow them to leave it.

Lotzzy's fort consisted of one floor, with a roof terrace at the top, occupied by several concrete machine gun nests, and a humid and unhealthy basement in which the troop's bedrooms, those of the officers, were located. as: such as food and ammunition depots.

Karl paid a detailed visit to the latter, noting with satisfaction that they were full and that, therefore, he guaranteed the nutrition of his men and that of his weapons for quite a long time.

The Russians were still far away and the captain dedicated that truce to reinforcing the fort's defenses, thickening the embrasures on the first floor with sandbags and establishing a fire plan that was as effective as possible.

The men had realized what was going to be demanded of them, and they all had an idea that those dirty walls had more than one chance of becoming his grave. But, carried away by the smiling character of their captain, they immediately abandoned the black thoughts of the beginning, letting themselves be carried away among the thousand occupations of the day and enjoying the tranquility that the distance of the enemy allowed them.

But everything ends ...

The arrival of the Soviet aviation was like a warning that the quiet days were gone. The huge four-wheelers bombed the entire strip of land that formed the isthmus between the two banks of the river. (The fort received its corresponding dose of explosives and five men lost their lives, attempting to machine-gun the bombers as they skimmed past.)

From that moment, the incursions became more numerous and Trauber had to take measures to prevent those attacks from causing him more casualties. Not having antiaircraft artillery, he preferred to lock himself in the basement with his boys, patiently waiting for the bombardment to end before returning to the outside. The walls of the fortress were strong enough not to fear that a bomb would cause the complete destruction of the redoubt.

Two days later, tranquility and silence once again took over the earth and the sky. But there was something sinister and false about this tranquility and silence that could in no way fool veteran combatants like the men of the Trauber Company.

There was not the slightest whisper, and even the waters of the river seemed to flow cautiously, fearfully, through the shifting branches of the swamps. The breeze had fled and the air, despite the low temperature, undoubtedly weighed on bodies and even more on souls.

It was an indefinite sensation in which the proximity of the definitive tragedy was "chewed"; something like a premonition, a foretaste, etched in the air, of the dangers that an ever closer horizon hid.

The nervous tension reached unsuspected limits and in the faces of the soldiers you could clearly read the concern that arises before the unknown whose power cannot be calibrated until it appears.

The time had come "of this there was no doubt for Karl" to speak seriously to the men. Then, later, in the heat of combat, words would be unnecessary and it was necessary for each of the soldiers to be impregnated with the quality of effort and sacrifice that were going to be demanded of them,

In the midst of that impressive silence, the captain made his men line up in the room that formed, almost entirely, the main floor of the fort.

"You feel in the air that they are getting closer, eh? "Were his first words, while smiling." Yes, my friends, the stench of Ivan is already everywhere. Although we have not yet managed to see their dirty faces, I am more than sure that their patrols are filling their eyes with our fortress "he paused and after walking through the tight ranks of the soldiers with a look of confidence.

"For the first time," he continued, "we are going to fight alone. No Unit to the right, no Unit to the left and nothing behind; a void that we cannot count on. Alone before an enemy a thousand times more powerful than us, but that has the disadvantage of being forced to penetrate the fort to break through to the West. I am not a friend of speeches and less on these occasions when the panorama that is offered to us is not at all promising. We've fought together long enough that we don't have to give each other stupid warnings.

"However" a sad smile accentuated the lines on his tired face "I would like to tell you that, whatever happens, I have full confidence that you will show the Soviets that the road to Berlin is not, far from it, a military walk. I am nobody to tell you about how the war is going; You already see that for yourselves and you comment on it sufficiently during the long watches or when sleep does not want to come. I assure you that I would prefer you to think like me who, I swear, I have forgotten everything, except that I am a German soldier who must not rest until the enemy surrenders or a bullet prevents me from continuing to fight ... "he made a new pause and then, with that smile with which he could achieve anything from his men ". Nothing else guys!

The soldiers withdrew in silence, but their eyes shone with the intensity of the good times when it was necessary to make an effort, almost always crowned with the only victory a soldier can hope for: death ...

CHAPTER TWO

"SEMUROW"

Not far from the Soviet General Staff, a dozen wide tents raised their dirty cones above the ground covered with trampled snow, which formed a blackish mud. Some men, sporting brand-new Thompson portable machine guns, recently arrived from the United States, guarded this group of stores against general curiosity.

However, it would not have been necessary for the guards to walk around doing their watch; no soldier would have dared get too close to the tiny camp, even if it was completely devoid of sentries.

Everyone knew, too well, the sad fame of Semurow. And while no Soviet soldier gave a damn what this man did with the Germans, the "secondary" missions that had been entrusted to Semurow during the great German offensive had made them aware of the partisan's savage instincts.

Semurow and his men had dedicated themselves, by superior orders, to preventing their frightened compatriots from fleeing before the impetuous German attack. And in the same way that the Germans who fell into their hands, ended up hanged; the Soviets that showed a certain speed in the retreat, fell under the bullets of the partisans, remaining in the snow as an example for those who forgot their duty.

Semurow had a huge ascendancy in the Army and even in the General Staff. In reality, the feelings they experienced were, perfectly camouflaged, those of fear; a logical fear of that angry panther who was not happy if he did not shoot someone.

In his cylindrical tent, Igor Semurow quietly smoked, surrounded by his "officers." He was tall, lanky, bony, yet broad-shouldered and of a nervous type of musculature. He had a narrow forehead, shaggy eyebrows, and an aquiline nose that vaguely recalled his Armenian origin.

The blackness of his eyes was perhaps the most sinister detail of his personality, since it was very difficult to find a similar color in any human face. That made him look like a butcher animal always on the lookout for helpless prey. In reality, few, very few were the men who dared to meet his piercing and keen gaze. And even those who dared did not like to do it without feeling an involuntary shudder run down their spines.

"Comrade Semurow" who was speaking was a kind of gorilla with a face that vaguely reminded that of a man ", it has been a long time since the offensive has started, that we do not do anything funny. These of the General Staff are fattening us like pigs ...

Igor looked at his interlocutor. He was one of her favorite men because of the bestiality he possessed.

"You are right, Trupiew. And I'm starting to get sick of all this. It is a real shame that the Germans flee like women! How I would like the Nazis to launch another of their offensives ...! So we did have a good time! Don't you think, Commissioner?

The questioned man, who was devouring the contents of a large can of meat, raised his head, giving a growl that was the only thing that could come out of his full mouth.

He must have been as tall as Trupiew himself, although his strength was more contained in a body that did not reach the seismic dimensions of the other, but that nevertheless possessed an animality and an evident primitivism.

His broad face was almost circular, in a spherical head of cropped hair and with the racial characteristics of the Orientals. Slanting eyes, huge flattened nose and prominent cheekbones, all in dumpy proportions, as if it were a sculpture made quickly, carelessly, like a sketch of a man in which the human was represented bestially.

No one knew his name, and none of the Semurow men understood a single word of the few that the "commissar" could utter. The story of his "appointment" by Igor was still the cause of laughter when someone told it among the bloody anecdotes of the group of partisans.

This man had been detained along with many more of his race as they fled swiftly before the German forces in a Southern Sector of the Eastern front. On that occasion, the Semurow group left the fields full of bodies of Uzbeks, in one of the missions of "discipline" to which they dedicated themselves with a special fervor.

It was on that occasion that, hidden in some bushes, they discovered that species of primitive man who growled, when discovered, like any wild animal chased by a pack of dogs.

When Trupiew was about to "kill" him, Semurow, who was with him, found all the growling amusing. At the same time, his keen eyes realized that underneath that expressionless face, there was a primitive man's ferocity that could be used properly oriented.

Raising his voice, at the same time that he grabbed Trupiew's armed arm to prevent him from firing.

"High! Let him out.

The Usbeko, at the imperative gesture of that man, came out of his precarious hiding place, letting his fleshy and thick lips draw an outline of a smile that looked more like a grotesque grimace with which he tried to disguise his fear.

He said something in his language that, of course, no one understood. Then, to make his surrender more effective, he raised his arms, placing both hands on the massive nape of his neck.

Semurow's men had gathered around their boss. Accustomed to amusing themselves with Igor's witticisms, almost always bloody, they hoped, on that occasion, to have a good time.

"Comrades! "Shouted Semurow with that sinister accent that his people liked so much." Here is the second leader of our group. You only have to look at him, to see that he is one of the greatest intelligences that we have encountered in the entire war "with a falsely solemn voice and trying to silence the laughter that exploded everywhere." I, Igor

Semurow, an independent partisan, appoint this man "commissioner" of my Group.

Since then, the "commissioner", who had not understood a single word of his boss's speech, was losing his fear as he was testing the taste of a food that he had not tasted in his entire existence.

Slowly, the son of the plains of Central Asia, he was assuring himself an existence as he could never have dreamed, becoming the faithful dog of Igor to whom he blindly obeyed. Semurow had seen, when choosing that Asian in the complex and vague, at the same time, the role of "commissioner." Thus, when one of the men in the Group forgot their duties, the chief pointed him out to the Usbeko and with a voice that did not admit any reply:

"Take care of him, 'Commissar', he's a filthy pig and traitor!

Then, in the yellowish background of those pupils that had seen nothing but sun-scorched plains and tiny horses, almost like dogs, they lit up with a terrible light of fierceness and the wretch who had been pointed out by Igor, felt, however in a short time, the Asian's claws close on his neck.

Outside of those "executive services", the "commissioner" spent his life trying to quench the hunger that, for long and terrible months, he had suffered from the front until he fell into the hands of the partisan.

Pending the lips of his "master" since within his primitive brain there was no difference between Semurow and the former owners of the country that his parents and their parents had known and served, the Usbeko consumed an incalculable quantity of cans of meat that the Semurow Group possessed in an amount that would have made any Red Army Unit die of envy.

So were Semurow and his men.

* * *

The first Russian soldiers appeared on the other side of the river ...

They were the vanguards of a powerful Army that had been entrusted with the mission of crossing Lotzzy to make contact with another that was advancing through the South. The union had to be carried out next to the old German-Polish border and, from that very moment, the Soviet troops could already be considered in full Germany

From the embrasures of the fort, Trauber's men were carefully examining the arrival of the first enemies. An unspoken silence reigned on both sides and only, like invisible projectiles, the looks, charged with hatred, were the only thing that crossed between both sides.

Leaning on the sandbags that had replaced the concrete destroyed by one of the Soviet aviation bombings, the captain watched carefully, with his binoculars, those rapid figures moving carefully along the opposite bank of the river.

The Russians wore padded uniforms and fur hats, the side extensions of which almost completely covered their faces. In their hands shone the modern weapons they had received from their western allies and they were no longer, as at first, barefoot and half-naked. His feet were protected by leather boots made not far from London ...

Throughout the day, the silhouettes walked along the banks of the river, digging with long sticks into the areas where the quicksand of the swamps closed, in an embrace of death, over everything that fell into them.

As night fell, Karl doubled the watch and kept his men on alert, waiting in vain for the enemy to initiate some offensive trial-and-error action.

The part of the fort that faced the river had been completely cleared of the remains of the blown-up bridge and offered nothing but the slick, slick surface of a "glacis" over which it was almost impossible for a man to climb. This was, in fact, the best defense available to the captain, since the aquatic plants abounded in this place, making the adventurous ascent of the enemy infantry even more difficult.

These, to reach the fort, should use landing craft or, failing that, pneumatic boats, since the depth of the river, although not excessive, had, on the contrary, the danger of a bottom formed by quicksand.

During the night, Trauber could not fall asleep, preferring to stroll on all sides of the fort, carefully going through the guards and constantly encouraging the sentries who invented to pierce the darkness that surrounded them.

Very soon, well before dawn, the opposite shore was lit up by hundreds of bonfires that demonstrated the arrival of all the troops ready to fight.

It was clear that the enemy knew, with some accuracy, the meager number of Germans guarding the fort and even the nature of their weapons. Certain, therefore, that they could swim that handful of German soldiers, they displayed and flaunted their strength, in front of an enemy that they planned to destroy in a minimum amount of time.

Thoughtfully, Karl surveyed the Russians, intimately convinced that the coming fighting was going to be exceptionally tough. He had full confidence in his soldiers, but he was not blind to the wild conclusion that they could resist an enemy of this category indefinitely.

Quickly counting the number of fires and applying a simple calculation, the German captain came to the conclusion that the forces stationed on the opposite bank of the river amounted to approximately the strength of a Soviet Division. Naturally, the Russians could have lit a number of bonfires that did not correspond to their true need. Such a contraption was already well known to all who had fought in the East.

But, in any case, logic would not fail to show that the Russians had brought in considerable forces, not to fight against the fort, precisely, but to continue the advance and carry out the occupation of the extensive Polish area that extended behind Lotzzy.

Dawn caught Karl watching the Soviet fire. As the daylight blurred the outline of the flames of the bonfires, the captain could glimpse the dense groups of soldiers warming themselves to the fu-ego.

He had not been mistaken.

There, on the other side of the filthy mass of the river, was an entire Division. Now you could see, not only the men, but the weapons; batteries located on the left; the tanks in the background, with their great brown masses and the elegant tents in which, without a doubt, the General Staff of the Unit was installed.

The Russians did not wait long. At eight o'clock in the morning, a destructive fire began against the fort. At one shot per second, the artillery began to sweep away with its horrible fire, the German defense.

After suffering the first casualties, Karl promptly ordered his men to descend into the cellar. Since the aviation had attacked so viciously, the captain had made two small holes drilled in the wall of the cellars, which revealed the entire forced passage of the river.

For six interminable hours, the artillery fire shook even the foundations of the solid building. The dust of the walls that were smashed to pieces and the smell of the trilite, descended through the interstices, making the atmosphere of the cellars was becoming frankly unbreathable.

(The three men who had been wounded by the first rounds of the enemy artillery ceased to exist around noon. Nothing could be done to prevent those enormous wounds from bleeding. deceive anyone. They were the first dead in the fort after those fallen in the bombardment. A macabre announcement for the heroic defenders who, looking askance at the immobile bodies of their companions, easily imagined that this would be, sooner or later, its logical end.)

In the course of the first hours of the afternoon and almost until dusk, an absolute tranquility reigned on the part of the Russians. The artillery had ceased firing and the silence, after the terrible uninterrupted storm of gunfire, seemed to upset the nerves far more than the cannon fire itself.

With his face pressed to one of the observation holes in the basement, the captain watched the enemy shore where, for the moment, everything remained immobile. With some bitterness, he recalled that not a single shot had been fired from the fort. Only the Soviets had spoken until then.

Suddenly...

The red shore began to tingle intensely. Hundreds of men were approaching the water's edge, carrying long inflatable canoes on their backs that they hurled into the water. Almost immediately and in the reddish light of sunset, a score of ships plowed through the waters in the direction of the fort.

Come on, guys, they're coming!

There was not the slightest sign of alarm in the German soldiers. On the contrary, a wild joy seized them at the announcement of the combat. They were tired of resisting a situation that was not at all brilliant and they preferred, a thousand times, to die killing enemies than to do it the way they had fallen to comrades during the artillery action.

They swiftly climbed to the top of the fort. At the sight of this chaotic pile of dirt and stones, they gave a willful exclamation of nasty surprise. Everything was changed there into a messy chaos into which the artillery had turned the upper defenses of the fort.

In no time, the Germans threw themselves on the rubble, preparing, in a few seconds, a place from which they could shoot comfortably.

Behind them and next to the captain, Lieutenant Lukas was personally in charge of setting the fire of the only two mortars they possessed.

The black barrels of the machine guns peeked over the stones and the crosshairs, covered the moving targets that were the inflatable boats.

Trauber allowed the enemy to enter the course of the river, until the boats were no more than a dozen meters from the elusive "glacis" of the fort. At that moment, with his own machine gun, he gave the signal to fire, firing at the Soviets himself.

The first inflatable boat, pierced by Trauber's accurate shots, took only a few seconds to sink. But, the Russians were very close to the lower part of the "glacis" and in a couple of energetic strokes, they reached the stones, preparing to climb the slope to reach the fort.

The other boats suffered the same fate, except for two that, under accurate mortar fire, blew up with all their crew.

That was precisely what Captain Trauber wanted ...

If it had not been for the tragic situation, the desperate efforts of the Russians, trying in vain to scale the slippery surface of the sloping wall that formed the "glacis", would have seemed extremely comical.

However, swept away by German bullets, which the Germans fired from twenty meters above, the Soviets collapsed heavily in the water, leaving behind a red stain that seemed to float for a few moments on the surface of the river before dissolving. completely.

Those who, panicking, tried the width of the river, swimming, suffered a worse death. Dragged downstream in the area of quicksand where they disappeared amid horrible screams that demonstrated the horrendousness of their horrifying agony.

When the last enemy had disappeared under the waters, the Germans, moved by a unison gesture of victory, gave a cry in which the joy was expressed in a noisy way. They had not suffered a single casualty, destroying, on the contrary, an entire Company that was the one that had tried in vain to take the fort by storm.

During the night, one of the Sections listened attentively. But when dawn came and the Soviet artillery began its violent bombardment, in retaliation for what happened the day before, the Germans quietly retired to the cellars, their hearts filled with joy.

Only Karl, while resting, trying to achieve a dream that was more than necessary, did not participate in the revelry of his men, knowing that the terrible hours of testing were only just beginning.

And of that he could be sure, he was not mistaken ...

CHAPTER THREE

THREAT AT NIGHT

Sitting opposite the general, Igor Semurow was calmly smoking one of the luxurious cigarettes with which the army chief had just given him.

The sharp eyes of the partisan did not separate from the face of his Interlocutor. The latter, visibly uncomfortable under that insistent gaze and lack of the slightest concept of respect and discipline, internally cursed the capricious order he had just received from Moscow and which, for him, constituted nothing more than a direct insult to the military forces under his command and indirectly, an affront to himself.

Squinting, to escape that intolerable gaze that had irremediably fixed on his pupils, the general recalled the hurtful paragraphs of the order that he had received directly from the Kremlin.

"Urgently needing to employ the forces under his command in the Northern Sector of the front and having shown his little fighting spirit, failing before a small number of enemies in the Lotzzy Sector, we order him to hand over complete control of said sector to the Paramilitary Forces of Colonel Semurow, which we are sure, will carry out victorious and swiftly the operation entrusted to him. His three Divisions will head towards the North Sector. to the GPU Field, closest to receive the appropriate framing and political teachings. "

Remembering that last paragraph, the general shuddered from head to toe.

"To receive the appropriate framing and political teachings" - "he repeated more slowly than the first time.

This meant that the Division would be decimated, after witnessing the mass execution of its officers and that, from that moment on, they would be replaced by elements of the Soviet police who would not let a single day pass without applying the death penalty to whom it deviated the least from what the GPU understood by "Soviet discipline."

The general opened his eyes again, daring this time to look at the man before him. Ever since he had left the Novegorod Military Academy, he had never even imagined that a war would take the special shape in which this one was unfolding.

Looking at Semurow, that "colonel" so esteemed in the upper middle of Moscow, the general thought bitterly of the time and life he had unfortunately lost with books. All the efforts in which he honestly launched himself with the intention of becoming an excellent military soldier, had not been more than the most obvious demonstration that the exercise of arms in his country was nothing more than something petty and secondary. , always subject to a policy that entirely dominated the command cadres.

There it was, sitting across from him, the clearest example of what he was thinking. A man without culture, without scruples; a bloodthirsty tiger of sorts, sporting the insignia of a colonel, a post to which he had passed directly from his obscure partisan post.

"Comrade Semurow" the effort he made to address that monster was unspeakable. " Moscow has ordered me to order the raid on Lotzzy's blockhouse. All our efforts have been completely useless, given the special tactical circumstances of that battlefield.

Igor tossed the cigarette butt to the ground, then crushing it with his rough mujik boots.

"Bullshit! "He coldly shot at the general's face." All of you are poisoned by strange words that you have learned in books as useless as your uniforms. To wage war, you don't need words, but actions. The enemy does not surrender more than when the boot is placed on his neck or the bayonet is sunk to the entrails ... all that "tactics" and "strategy" does not serve more than to chat in the warm rooms of your Academies ...

The general felt the blush rise to his face, whipping it like a blast of fire. Biting her lip, she tried to forget what she had just heard.

"Everyone has their own way of waging war, Comrade Semurow," he replied in a voice veiled by anger. But we have not come here to argue among ourselves, but to see the best way to end up sinking the common enemy. What weapons do you need for the assault?

"None! Igor's voice was one of intolerable insolence. In recent years, no one has asked me what weapons I needed to hang the Nazis. My men and I, we know perfectly well that the Germans are not frightened by cannons and aviation. Those dogs need special treatment to understand that they must leave Russia! "He stood up and gave his interlocutor a look of contempt": Save the weapons, the cannons, the planes and the tanks, for your soldiers who cannot wage war without "tactics" or "strategy"! And tell them, for me, on behalf of Igor Semurow, that they are a gang of sluts, cowards like their bosses and that my men will show them how to take a fort with open chests to enemy bullets.

The general had risen to his feet. Pale as a dead man, his right hand swiftly lowered to where his pistol holster hung. But the calmness of his arrogant visitor, who did not even blink, and the fear of what would happen next, when Moscow learned that he had killed "Colonel Semurow", stopped him as he thought of his wife and little daughter who were eagerly awaiting his triumphant return ...

* * *

The Germans couldn't believe what they were seeing with their own eyes ...

On the opposite bank, the Soviet troops, in correct formation, were heading towards a very long line of trucks in which they were climbing in small groups.

Powerful tractors also came to drag the heavy artillery pieces and the column, endless like a trail of ants, soon disappeared into the distant horizon, leaving behind a dust cloud that rose towards the sky, finally dissolving completely.

The soldiers expressed their joy with cheers and hugs. Their voices sounded in the fort like cries of resounding victory. It seemed indeed, on seeing them, that the war had just ended with a resounding triumph for the Third Reich.

Trauber was smiling too ...

However, as soon as he could, he abandoned his soldiers and, accompanied by Lieutenant Lukas, descended into the cellars in the small room that belonged to him.

Lukas was a blond giant, the classic pure Nordic racial type, with athletic builds and a narrow forehead. Her blue eyes were full of life and her thin lips were adorned, almost constantly, with a smile in which there seemed to reside an Olympian contempt for danger.

They sat on the blankets that served as the captain's bed.

"You don't believe them, eh, sir?

"What do I have to believe, Lukas?

"Let the Russians really go ...

Trauber looked intently at the officer. Later:

"I don't think there is any doubt that they are leaving, Lieutenant. It would be absurd to imagine that they are performing a maneuver to deceive us. You will understand that for a handful of men like we are, they are not going to generate the gasoline for all those trucks.

They were silent for a while. Finally, the lieutenant made up his mind to probe his superior. Thus, frankly and openly.

"I would like to know what you think of all this, Captain.

"It's very easy, Lukas," replied Karl with a smile. The Russians are gone, that is an undeniable reality. But, if they have left the game, it has been by verifying that, with the methods they have used, the fort would never fall into their hands, or it would take long enough that it would no longer be useful to occupy it. You must not forget, Lieutenant Lukas, that, both in the North and in the South, about a hundred kilometers from here, on both sides, ours are fighting desperately before an enemy superior in everything. By the time these two opposing Armies advance a little, approximately three hundred kilometers, Lotzzy will have ceased to exist as a military necessity.

"Does that mean that we will have to withdraw?

"I do not believe it. Advancing three hundred kilometers in front of a German Army that, although weak, resists bravely is not as simple as taking this fort and taking our troops from behind. You may have noticed that the Russians, since they began their series of offensives, have adopted as their own the tactic that most of Europe gave us: the pincer.

"What I do not understand are the reasons for this enemy retreat. Yes, as you say, they are interested in seizing Lotzzy as soon as possible, I cannot explain why they left.

"Neither do I, Lieutenant. But don't worry, it won't be long before we know what's behind all this.

Except for the group that stood guard in the upper part of the fortress, the rest of the Company rested from the weary hours of combat. The men slept soundly, forgetting, for a few hours, the historical and personal tragedy in which they had been for years.

That night, Sergeant Kopler was with the entirety of his platoon watching from the ruined battlements, the blackness of the Russian night that enveloped them. Silence and darkness had become completely twinned since the Russians had withdrawn from the opposite shore. Nothing seemed to disturb the tranquility of that Polish corner; as if the dead of many ages and of many wars had, at last, won for them a silence that seemed to become eternal.

Kopler went from one sentry to another, chatting a little with each one and putting in their apparently inconsequential words a thorn of hope that did not fail to encourage the boys.

One of the times, when he spoke to one of them, he was suddenly silent, trying to pierce the darkness through which the waters of the river ran.

It was evident that, above the noise of the current, another, different, interrupted one could be heard, as if someone was desperately stroking there. If it was a swimmer, the sound that reached the sergeant's ears came from a single human being who was drowning or, on the contrary, who was trying, in a colossal effort, to reach the fort.

The singularity of the sound made Kopler not decide to raise the alarm. If it was, as he was almost certain, a mad enemy or a German who had managed to cross the Russian lines, desperately throwing himself into the river, he alone could solve the problem. Furthermore, the prospect of capturing a prisoner was extremely tempting.

After confiding to the sentry what he intended to do and ordering him to cover his retreat, Kopler gently descended the "glacis", using a rough path that he had learned by heart from the beginning.

He descended like a shadow among the shadows, silent and caring, all ears and aware of the soft whisper that kept coming from the river. As she approached shore, the assurance that someone was swimming, already close to her, was completed by a kind of gasping growl from the mysterious character.

When the sergeant's feet touched the flat ledge where the "glacis" ended, already in the water, he froze completely at the sound of the man's gasping breathing and the sound of water falling from his soaked clothes.

The stranger must have been very close to him and Kopler, pistol in one hand and flashlight in the other, made up his mind to act. The most important thing was not to miss the blow, since he could not afford to light the lantern more than once and, furthermore, the fight on that little stone ledge would have been impossible.

He switched on the flashlight, in a quick flash, as he delivered the blow with the butt of the pistol. It all happened in a fraction of a second and the sergeant had to move quickly to prevent the body of the man he had just deprived of consciousness from falling into the water.

Holding him with his arms and legs, in an awkward position, Kopler could not help but consider himself happy to have accomplished something so uncertain and difficult. Then, raising his head towards the fort:

"Hans! "scream". Throw a rope! Let two more help you.

It didn't take long for him to feel the rope brush against him as he fell from above. Skillfully, he bound the prisoner's body, ordering it to be hoisted.

They did so, again throwing the rope to raise the sergeant. The wall was excessively elusive and Kopler had to allow himself to climb, pretending to be dead, since on the part where they were hoisting him, there was not the slightest edge that could be used to help the ascent:

The soldiers had left the body of the man captured by their superior stretched out, waiting to receive the appropriate instructions from him.

"Take him downstairs," he ordered. In the meantime I am going to wake up the captain.

In the common room, lit by oil lanterns, Karl carefully examined the prisoner's motionless body.

He is a Usbeko ", he clarified after realizing the racial group of that man". This, if I am not mistaken, means that we have been placed in front of the most barbarous of Russian soldiers. The guard will have to be strengthened, because, as we have just seen, these people nothing like fish.

The Usbeko had begun to half open his eyes. His pupils perked up intensely and, shaking his head, he cast a circular glance around. Then, understanding his situation, he let out a fierce growl.

"Who are you? Asked the captain.

The slanting eyes locked with Trauber's. Afterwards and as it had been asked in Russian:

"I'm the commissioner," he replied.

Karl realized that the man could not speak Russian and that the words he had just spoken were perhaps the only ones he had learned after enormous efforts. However, he asked the other question that was more important to him and his people than the first.

"Who's your boss?

The other did not take his gaze from the captain's face. Hearing the second question, his torso expanded into an expression of unspeakable pride.

"Semurow! He replied.

CHAPTER FOUR

DARKNESS!

"Nitchevo" was very happy ...

For the first time in her life that she could say had not brought her any joy, the young woman's heart knew the delicious taste of a hope that she had anchored in her heart with such an intense force that it served, alone, to metamorphose the girl's existence.

She had almost come to forget the strange silence that took hold of her when she attended the murder of her father for ... But, she preferred to keep all that in the most forgotten corner of her memory, enjoying a present that had made her know moments of a joy unknown, until then for her.

The existence in Tepluja, since the arrival of the Germans who had been in charge of the occupation of the town, was for her, calm and peaceful. The document that Captain Trauber had made for her made things extremely easy for her, being respected by all and enjoying perfect treatment and deference, in addition to the fact that every week, she was given a supply of food, enough to be able to live without worries. .

"Nitchevo" was not, however, one of the women who can stand idly by and, through the eloquent gestures that she used to make herself understood, she let the occupants know that she was willing to worry about the condition of their clothes. , as he had done with the men of the Trauber Company.

Everyone in Tepluja adored it and nothing was missing from their table, since the Germans had found in it something simply non-existent in the distance that separated them from their homes. If ever anyone came close to forgetting the girl's sanctity, her companions, and Karl's signature on the document, they acted as strong reminders, and things did not go beyond an aborted joke without the utmost importance.

In the emotional world of "Nitchevo", the only image that inhabited, owner of all his thoughts, was that of Captain Trauber. She had to honestly confess that she had fallen in love with that German, whom she hardly knew. A thousand different doubts assailed her at the beginning and she had to fight fiercely against them, in order to continue building her future using as mortar a hope to which she had firmly attached the primary reason for her existence.

Karl and his men sent her some funny pictures, with short inscriptions that, although she did not understand, she guessed with her fine feminine instinct. At night, when she fell to her bed weary from her daily work, she prayed for those men who, in some far corner of the country, fought and died in the tremendous silence of frozen nights.

But, after the happy times of peace in that Russian rearguard, the bad times came ... Again the restlessness and fear were born in the aching heart of "Nitchevo" and the roldados that he saw singing towards the line of fire, They returned now, tired, dirty, many of them bandaged, wounded, with death in the dull glow of their pupils and a look of infinite sadness on their faces.

She was invited to go backwards. They kindly made room for her in a truck and the terrible exodus began, seeming to never end. New countries, unknown regions, in which he had never set foot, paraded before the sad eyes of "Nitchevo".

Everyone was still nice to her. But, little by little, as the conditions of the fronts became more precarious, when the facts of an undoubted defeat were nailed in the hearts of the Germans, the kindnesses gave way to the sullen glances, to the rare brightness in the eyes of men who ceased to be when death, within an unjust picture of lost war, gripped them with its icy arms.

"Nitchevo" realized that everything was turning, going bad and that a rare demonic action accompanied the despair of those who already feared the violation of their homes by the Soviets, the burning of their homeland and the eternal agony of a horrible slavery .

One night, silently, "Nitchevo" fled east with the only hope of finding Captain Trauber. Fate could not disappoint that heart in which purity, like a rare gem in those bloody moments, shone amid the desolation and evil that rode, in intimate company with the Four Horsemen of the Apocalypse. •

• • •

SEMUROW!

Once again, at the behest of cruel fate, the Trauber Company was face to face with the partisan. The Russian command had known how to entrust the attack on Lotzzy to a man who had a much better chance than any other to achieve it.

Trauber stared at the fallen body of the Usbeko. From that precise moment, he was fully convinced that the fight was going to take very different directions from those it had taken up to now.

There would be no more artillery preparation, brutal aviation attacks, no rubber boats trying to make their way to the fort. With Semurow you had to prepare for a hidden, terrible fight, without quarter, at any time, in any place and at any time.

It would be necessary to remain wide-eyed, day and night, without possible rest and without ever leaving a single man in any guard post. Karl knew his new enemy too well to let his men, one by one, adorn the trees, like ghoulish fruits, on the banks ahead.

On the one hand, he felt a kind of satisfaction knowing that Igor was on the other side of the river. They had many pending accounts to settle with that murderer and he only wished that the morale of his men would not yield to the curse of the word Semurow, so that he could erase from the world of the living that viper of which he knew so much ...

He had never wanted to say anything to anyone and continued to observe the documentation of the old man who died in the "isba" of

Tepluja, next to whose corpse "Nitchevo" cried inconsolably. But, on the rare occasions when he had read it again, he could not manage to digest the idea that there were men in whom the beast completely erased his category of humans.

Because that poor old man Andrei Semurow was none other than the father of that scoundrel who had undoubtedly been his murderer!

Karl had always suspected that "Nitchevo" was Igor Semurow's sister. But he had never been able to be sure, since the features of the dead old man had nothing like those of the young woman. On the other hand, having never seen the partisan, it was impossible for him to make a physiognomic comparison between him and the girl.

It could also be his girlfriend ... He had thought so many times, feeling the hatred he felt towards Semurow grow even more. But at the moment, he could not, in any way, prove either of the two hypotheses that were formulated.

The important thing now was to prepare for the fight against Igor and the soulless who made up his "patriotic" group. After having the "comisario" locked up in one of the fortress dungeons, Trauber summoned his officers, giving them an exact account of the situation.

"I have to give you news," he started to say. The Russians have sent us an old "friend" of the Company. I mean, for those who have not guessed his name Igor Semurow. It is he, now, who is going to be in charge of attacking this fort. It goes without saying that he will use every means at his disposal to destroy us. We already know that with him there will be no truce or prisoners ... "he paused and staring at his officers" I WANT US TO DO THE SAME ... an eye for an eye, a tooth for a tooth. It will be the law of Talión the one that reigns from this moment between us and the enemy. I will never tire of warning that there should not be a single forgetfulness, nor the slightest distraction in Lotzzy. Understood?

Throughout the next morning, the calm was too strange to spring from Igor's initiative. The Germans were restless, nervous, looking at the empty and deserted opposite bank and hoping that the enemy would rush to the assault as soon as possible.

There was something sinister about that silence, of tremendous waiting in which the eyes and the entire body came to be annihilated in a nervous tension that exhausts and destroys him completely.

All of this heralded the arrival of tragedy that finally erupted with chilling brutality.

It was Kramer, the one who had always acted as an assistant sergeant with Trauber, who, while on guard by the "glacis," descended toward the Command Post. The officers were meeting with the captain.

"What do you want, Kramer? "He inquired when he saw the sergeant.

"I wanted to ask Lieutenant Lukas which platoon was going to take over the night watch. Since it's getting dark, I thought it was time to ask.

Karl's eyes locked on the sergeant's face. Then, in an automatic gesture, he glanced quickly at the wristwatch. It was exactly ten past three.

"It's getting dark ..." "Kramer had said.

With a quick gesture so that the sergeant would not notice that signal, Trauber silenced the surprise of the others. Then, getting up, he approached the noncommissioned officer.

"It's very good, Kramer. With the lieutenant's permission, I will be the one to name the incoming platoon "after a pause in which he kept looking intensely at his interlocutor." I wish I would go up to the positions, Karl. Do you want to accompany me?

"Whatever you order, captain," the other rushed to reply.

It did not seem "in Trauber's judgment" to answer badly for the state of his mind. Because Karl was more than sure that the poor sergeant had lost his mind.

He ascended the ladder followed by the sergeant. Outside, the sun, though weak, still lent everything very bright. It was even more than two long hours until dusk.

Without comment, Trauber headed straight for the assembled parapets that faced the river. There, stretched out among the sandbags, the sentries, rifles in hand, constantly watched the opposite bank.

"What's up, guys? "Asked the captain jovially." Do you see a lot of Russians?

The men turned, touching the edge of the helmet respectfully. One of them, a big burly man, who couldn't hide his southern German origin, replied with a smile.

"With the darkness closing in on us, you can see very little now, sir.

A chill ran down Karl's spine. Immediately, he cast a glance towards the opposite shore where a great deal of detail could still be seen. Some empty tin cans, abandoned by the Soviets, glowed brightly like pieces of mirror, being slantedly wounded by sunlight.

Trauber, making an enormous effort to keep his cool, asked the soldiers of the guard, one by one, and obtained, in a categorical way, the same answer.

"I'm going to relieve you right away, Sergeant Kramer. I will send another platoon immediately.

He went down to the basements and after giving the appropriate orders personally, he went, heartbroken to his room where the officers were still waiting for him.

Closing the door and leaning on it as if afraid that his words might open it again, he said in a voice laden with unspeakable anguish.

"Our boys are going blind ...

***

Igor, comfortably installed in his tent, about four miles from the river bank, gazed with inhuman hatred at the shrunken figure in front of him.

Kupriew, with the machine gun in hand, did not miss a single movement of the man who, hunched over himself, trembled with terror as if he were in the middle of the frozen plain, surrounded by hungry wolves.

Semurow smoked those endless "papirossi" that, since the general had invited him, he had not missed a single moment more. A special courier from Moscow had brought him ten huge boxes, with a personal dedication from the Kremlin.

Through the bluish smoke from the long scented cigarettes, the malevolent eyes of the partisan seemed to express intimate joy. Actually, it was. Igor was delighted to find that, in his presence, men were so diminished that they seemed crawling inferior and cowardly beings who did not deserve a life they unjustifiably enjoyed. Because, for Semurow, the only valid thing was the decision and the joy to erase from the world of the living everything that was weak, sick or enemy.

Igor had read very little. In fact, when he did, he found it tremendously difficult to understand what the lyrics were expressing. But, endowed with a rare memory, he nevertheless remembered everything he heard and, mainly, the content, not totally digested, of the speeches that the "konsomoles" used to make on their short visits to Tepluja.

One of them had referred to the theories of a wise Englishman, who declared as axiomatic the struggle for existence in which the less perfect, the battered, the weak and, in general, the timorous, must necessarily fall in front of the strong , to those excellently endowed by Nature and who were like prototypes, the only survivors of the atrocious struggle for existence.

Those words were deeply etched in Semurow's obtuse mind, which eventually came to make them his own. Nothing seemed more logical to him than the expression of a fight in which the strong were, irrevocably, the victors.

For this reason, and while he looked with contempt at the man before him, he felt the hatred of his own power against the trembling figure of that peasant that one of his men had captured when he heard him speak of a certain gallery that passed under the river.

But that "mujik", moved by mysterious thoughts, had repented of his words, undoing himself once before Igor.

"I assure you I did not say that, comrade. Comrade soldier must have been mistaken ... I am sure he misinterpreted my words.

Igor allowed a little silence to pass. Then speaking slowly, gluttonously syllableing each word.

"We're going to gouge your eyes out, you dirty spy. Then we will make you look for the entrance to the gallery with sticks. Afterwards, we will feed you our dogs.

The "mujik" trembled from head to toe. Inside his poor brain, the few ideas he had, formed an absurd mixture, a kind of crazy hubbub from which he could not get anything clean.

"Take out his right eye, Kupriew!

He came forward threateningly.

The peasant, sensing the presence of the other, fell to his knees before Igor.

"Forgive me, father! I didn't mean to say that! Really, there is no such gallery! I swear to you, father!

"Take out his right eye, Kupriew !!

An inhuman scream tore through the silence that had followed Igor's tremendous words. Later, when the "mujik" collapsed unconsciously, making a gesture of displeasure towards his subordinate:

"Get this pig out of here, Kupriew! It's going to stain my carpet! "A pause", Ah! ... And when he is revived ... and clean, that they bring him back.

His orders were promptly obeyed. Then when Kupriew came back to him.

"Sit down, comrade! Have one of these delicious cigarettes. You will see what a wonderful aroma. It seems that they have been specially made to remove the smell of cow that that disgusting "mujik" has left behind. "He narrowed his eyes, looking between the bluish scrolls that he had just thrown through his nostrils." We will ever make it to Berlin, Kupriew!

Imagine that, my friend! They say that there are women so beautiful and so clean that you start to tremble when approaching them ... "she closed her eyes completely". We will go to Berlin. We will walk through its wide avenues, as the only true winners. The Germans will bow their necks as that miserable "mujik" has just done and the beautiful women will throw flowers at us from the windows, inviting us to enter the palaces to enjoy in their company. Imagine, Kupriew, what wonderful things! When have you dreamed, you disgusting louse, to enter a great city where everything is at your disposal? Well, thanks to Igor Semurow, you will. I promise you! You can start dreaming now, old comrade. Do you remember the life we led in Tepluja until the war broke out? I was cursing myself as I passed, before dawn, in front of the door of your father's smithy. I was cursing your father, your mother and all of yours, because you could allow them to get up two or three hours later than me ... I assure you that, laughs that I could, I would have burned down your house and the smithy, just to see you leave! the bed when I was going to work in the fields ... Do you remember, comrade? You can start dreaming now, old comrade. Do you remember the life we led in Tepluja until the war broke out? I was cursing myself as I passed, before dawn, in front of the door of your father's smithy. I was cursing your father, your mother and all of yours, because you could allow them to get up two or three hours later than me ... I assure you that, laughs that I could, I would have burned down your house and the smithy, just to see you leave! the bed when I was going to work in the fields ... Do you remember, comrade? You can start dreaming now, old comrade. Do you remember the life we led in Tepluja until the war broke out? I was cursing myself as I passed, before dawn, in front of the door of your father's smithy. I was cursing your father, your mother and all of yours, because you could allow them to get up two or three hours later than me ... I assure you that, laughs that I could, I would have burned down your house and the smithy, just to see you leave! the bed when I was going to work in the fields ... Do you remember, comrade?

Kupriew nodded.

"I was also cursing you and yours," he replied with his monotonous voice. You already know that your sister Irina was beautiful like a flower that bloomed by the river, through the snow. But you and yours always prevented me from getting close to her. And that is why, every time I saw you return with the team at dusk, I would have killed you so that, just once, you would not have arrived in town so early, when I still had, together with my father, three good hours of work.

Semurow sighed with the last puff of smoke.

"All that is the past, comrade and it must be forgotten as soon as possible! You are no longer a blacksmith, nor am I a peasant. We are leaders of the Red Army! ... "He paused as if he had forgotten the train of his thought." You know my weakness for Irina. The last time we were in Tepluja, I begged him to follow us. But she, after seeing me kill my father, who was nothing more than a disgusting reactionary, stayed there to die, surely, pierced by a Nazi bullet ...

Kupriew's eyes gleamed sinisterly.

"You already know that that Company is the one that is now on the other side of the river, right?

"I already know it! That is why I am preparing a series of surprises that, if they could stay alive, they would not immediately forget "he got up, kneeling on the carpet." Do you know what I want to do with them when we capture them, old comrade?

Kupriew shrugged.

"I am going to send their heads in socos to Moscow. I want those of the Kremlin, when they receive the package in one of those halls, which they say are the most luxurious in the world, to faint like sluts when they discover the contents "he gave a blood-curdling laugh." Can you imagine the scene, Kupriew? I have been told that the Moscow Communists bathe and perfume themselves every day like the beautiful women of Berlin.

"It must be true," replied the other. A comrade who was there told me that when the Nazis were so close, they raided a party commissary and that all men's underwear was made of silk.

The two of them laughed together, until tears welled up in their eyes.

Well, "Igor cut in once he managed to recover from the effects of laughter." Go find the "mujik" and see if he wants us to take out the other eye. I hope you have thought better of it.

Kupriew got up. He was already at the door of the store when he turned.

"I am remembering the" commissioner ". What do you think the Germans did to him?

"Nothing, I'm sure. They will have beaten you up to make a statement. But, you know that this Usbeko has a very hard head. He's a good boy! When I ordered him to take the gas jars to the fort, he did not wince. I already knew that there were cracks next to the water that led up to the parapets, next to some very old holes in the cement. At this hour, the gas will be entering from all sides and leaving those disgusting Nazis blind. Then I will send their heads to Moscow so that the silk-clad communists swoon ...

"Do you think that gas will not attack the" commissioner "?

"So ... if so? After all, if things had been as they should have been, you would have killed him when we found him. Come on, go find the "mujik"!

Moments later, the unfortunate peasant entered Semurow's tent, trembling as never before.

He didn't even look at him.

"Or you take us to the entrance of the gallery to take out the other eye.

The "mujik" dropped to his knees.

"Don't make me suffer more, father! With only one eye, I can still drive the team and gather the wheat. These lands that they have given us, in Poland, give a lot of wheat ... you know?

Igor jumped to his feet.

"Take out the other eye, Kupriew! He screamed out of himself.

"Not! I will tell you where the entrance to the gallery is located, which leads, under the river, to the basements of the fort. I will accompany you, comrades.

"It's okay. Go with him, Kupriew. Have some men join you. I want them to go as far as possible and to come back, immediately, to tell me what they have done.

Kupriew went out accompanying the "mujik" who, turning to Igor, thanked him for having saved him from the torture.

"I will pray to the icons every night for you, father!

Five minutes later, Kupriew returned

"We're leaving now, Semurow. What is to be done with the peasant after he has shown us the entrance to the gallery?

Hang him! Was the laconic reply.

CHAPTER FIVE

ANGUISH IN THE BLACK

The dreadful evening that Sergeant Kramer first felt spread to all the men of the Company ...

Those brave soldiers could do nothing when, following Trauber's instructions, they tried to close with rags, with mortar made of clay and with a thousand different things, the holes and interstices through which the tremendous blinding gas was seeping.

They all realized, too late, that Semurow had ignored the laws of war. For that outlaw, nothing existed that could oppose his plans. Besides, once the Trauber Company had disappeared ... Who would testify that the Russians had released gases?

Karl, overcoming the horrible and slow agony that was taking hold of his soul, tried, by all the means at his disposal, to show exceptional courage in the face of the misfortune that was beating down on them. Taking off the rest, he went from one place to another, instilling hope that, deep down, he did not feel at all.

He spoke to his men, stating categorically that this blindness would not last forever and that the damage caused by gas to the eyes was only temporary. But he was the first to not trust his own words.

Everything had changed in the fort. It seemed as if the courage of the men was turning into frank despair, in which duty had more overtones of inexorable death sentence than anything else.

The guards continued, day and night, in that eternal gloom, with their ears attentive to the slightest noise. They could no longer trust their eyes, and for them, the contours of things had slowly faded until they could only perceive a diffuse clarity populated by strange and unrecognizable objects.

They waited with rage and mixed desires for the moment of attack. When the bullets began to hiss above their heads, in the semi-invisible world around them, they would fight fiercely until the moment of death.

Despite the strenuous efforts that Trauber constantly made, he failed to wrest from his men that fatalism which had so deeply anchored in them. It was an intolerable situation, dreadful at all times, while waiting for the arrival of Semurow's men who would end the Company in a jiffy.

Despair!

An indefinable sensation, with a painful emotional intensity, in which you tremble and fear forty-eight hours a day. Every second that passed without anything strange happening, was like a century stolen from destiny that was shaping, cruelly, the disastrous end of that horrifying adventure.

For all the men of the Trauber Company, Lotzzy's outpost took on a name that suited him better than any other:

The Fort of Despair!

Thus they waited, at any moment, with their hair standing on end with terror, that the knotty hands of their enemies, from whom they could not expect any mercy, would definitely close on their necks ...

* * *

"There is the entrance to the gallery.

Leaving the peasant in the hands of the two men who held him tightly, Kupriew advanced towards the place where several rocks of regular size formed the entrance of a cave whose edges were supported with cement.

It must have been a gallery built by the Poles to cross the river under water, for a reason that the Russian could not and was not interested in explaining.

It was at that precise moment, as he approached the entrance to the gallery, that he saw a human shadow lying there, forming a dark mass, in contrast to the blackness of the cave.

Taking out the long knife from which he never parted, the Soviet crept forward, preparing to surprise the one who had had the terrible idea of falling asleep in that place.

Once he was next to the stranger, who was lying wrapped in a dirty blanket, he leaned down, pulling her brutally, as he prepared to drive the knife into his body, at the slightest suspicious movement.

But, his surprise was so great that, without realizing exactly what was happening to him, he let the weapon slip from his hand, falling to the ground where it rang loudly. Then, in a hoarse voice, broken by emotion:

"Irina!

Irina Semurow, the "Miss Nitchevo" for the Germans, widened her eyes, widening them from the terror she felt. Later, like a whisper, as unpleasant memories arise and that are believed to have been buried forever in oblivion.

"Kupriew!

He had recovered his speech a couple of weeks ago, in the same calm way that he lost it in distant Tepluja. But the sad experience was almost repeated, when he met someone he never thought to see again.

"Yes, it's me, Irina dear. Kupriew, the man who has never stopped loving you ...

She was trembling like a tree leaf shaken by a strong gale. He kept looking, wide-eyed, at that inopportune apparition of a past that he wanted to forget for good.

"Wait for me here a bit, Irina. I'll come right away ... I promise you.

The young woman was on guard.

"Are you going to warn my brother?

Kupriew shook his head vigorously from side to side.

"You think I'm crazy? If Igor knew you here, I would lose you forever. And, now that I have been lucky enough to find you, I will never let anyone separate me from you.

The Russian's eyes were bright with desire. She turned or shuddered. But, above his terror, a hope was making its way into the terrible chaos that reigned in his brain.

The Soviet walked away. Irina, wrapping herself with the blanket, kept thinking, unable, for the moment, to find a solution that would suit her. But at least he had managed to avoid a painful and frightening encounter with his brother.

When Kupriew returned, he sat next to her, placing a can of meat and a canteen of "vodka" on the blanket.

"You must be hungry, poor thing!

She smiled at him, quietly eating. It was true that hunger gripped her and for that reason, she finished with the contents of the can, refusing, on the contrary, to taste alcohol.

"I had a drink in the river a while ago. Thanks Kupriew "and after a short pause": What are you doing here?

He smiled happy to see how well things were going. At that moment, his hatred for Semurow was increasing rapidly.

"We are going to attack the fort on the other side of the river. But don't worry, popcorn. There are very few enemies there and we will kill them in no time. Think what a single Company, already decimated, against us means!

"A German Company only? She inquired with mock admiration.

"Yes. It's the famous Trauber Company ..._ but it doesn't matter.

She had to lean on the ground, with both hands, to avoid the fading that was rapidly taking over her entire being. Then it was true! The German soldiers who had informed her, about a hundred kilometers back, when she crossed the river on an Engineers pontoon, had not been wrong to tell her that Trauber was in Lotzzy. Joy and sadness were intimately mixed in his soul.

Kupriew, believing to interest her with his bravado, continued to expose Semurow's plan to take over the fort.

"We have discovered a gallery through which we will enter the cellars. Those Nazi pigs are in for a nice surprise.

For her there was nothing else, in the imminent future, but to warn the man she loved of the danger that loomed over him and his soldiers.

How many would be left of the ones she had met?

He had indelible memories of those boys whom he had come to regard as brothers. It was the most exciting page of a life that was, fully, full of bitterness.

"I have to go back to camp, Irina. And I don't want any of your brother's men to see you. You can hide around here, since we are going to use the gallery. It will take very little time to pierce the end which, we have been told, is completely closed. Then everything will pass quickly and soon I will return to your side. That will be the time to leave Semurow for good. We're going to live in a place where your filthy brother can never find us.

She nodded. He wanted that disgusting individual to get away from there as soon as possible. He could not, no matter how hard he put forth, feel the slightest compassion for Kupriew, for the glint of desire in his eyes expressed the only kind of love that could be expected of him.

The Russian drew his pistol and handed it to the young woman.

"Here, Irina. If someone wants to annoy you ... Kill them! It will be better for him if you don't hurt him badly, as I would cut him to pieces. Now ... "his voice became intensely hoarse." ... give me a kiss, beautiful.

"Nitchevo" avoided the nausea by sheer miracle. When his lips finally parted from hers, she sighed in relief.

Once alone, not much rest time was allowed. He wanted to get to the other side of the river as soon as possible. But his original project, having passed through the gallery, had collapsed when he learned, through Kupriew, that there was no direct communication with the fort.

I had to swim across the river. At this idea, he shuddered, since he had heard some peasants whom he encountered before reaching the mouth of the gallery speak of the fearsome quicksand that delimited the sides of a narrow area of water, devoid of such danger.

She would have to stay in the center, fighting incessantly against the treacherous current that would push her into the sands that James could emerge from.

It wasn't fear that worried her. At least the fear of losing his life. What she feared, in reality, was not being able to warn her friends in time, saving them from a death, which when she remembered the soldiers hanging from the trees of Tepluja, made her shudder again.

With a wonderful decision, she placed the pistol in a handkerchief she wore, then knotted it tightly around her head. Then, without further hesitation, he began to walk toward the area in front of the fort.

It was dusk when he entered the water. Before doing so, she prayed to God that the Germans would not mistake her for an enemy and kill her in the middle of the river. But, in addition, she trusted that before pulling against her they would observe her with the twins.

The water was almost freezing and Irina took a long time to react, swimming vigorously and without hanging, as a crosshair, the gray "glacis" of Lotzzy's fortress.

For about an hour he was fighting bravely against the powerful current that incessantly pulled his body towards the area of quicksand. Finally, and when he thought he would soon give way to fatigue, he managed to take hold of some aquatic grasses that sprouted from the lower part of the stony slope.

"High!

He heard the voice, as the first projectiles hissed dangerously around him like angry bees.

Half dead with fear, she made a supreme effort and, drawing strength from weakness, screamed until she was hoarse.

"I am" Nitchevo "...! I'm "Nitchevo" ...! Call Captain Trauber ...!

* * *

Lieutenant Lukas was stumbling down the stairs that led to the captain's room. Twice in a row, he nearly fell. But, in his blindness, he had already begun, like all the men of the Company, to march with arms spread out in places that they already knew in detail.

"Captain Trauber ...! Captain Trauber!

Karl, who had already heard the fire of the rifles, was rushing out of his little room. The moment of combat seemed to have arrived and he and Trauber clenched their fists, hoping that, if death reached him, he could, at least, die with his hands clasped on the neck of his hated enemy.

"Captain Trauber!

Karl's voice took on a harsh tone. It annoyed him that men and even officers since blindness had wounded them, were becoming weak, lazy beings, compared to the tough soldiers they used to be.

"I already heard the shots, Lieutenant!

But the other, ignoring the harsh tone of the captain, came to his side, and finding him, at the end of his trembling hands, cut him short with irresistible force.

"But," Karl protested. What the hell is wrong with him, Lukas?

"Miss" Nitchevo "has arrived, my captain! It was she who alarmed the men on the parapets. They are hoisting it now!

Trauber felt his heart begin to beat with unusual fury as a fiery blush burned his cheeks. Hand in hand with the officer, he climbed the stairs as quickly as he could, when he reached the top, the animated conversations of the soldiers made him even more excited.

Suddenly, a cry sounded by his side, then, without knowing how, the girl's arms encircled him, at the same time that he felt, again, those lips that were anxiously clinging to his.

"Karl dear!

Irina's tears burned her face.

"But ... how did you get here, girl?

After guiding him up the stairs and into his room, she explained everything to him in detail. The girl's eyes did not separate from those of the man she loved, while the words came from her tight lips so that he would not notice the tears that continued to carve her face.

Karl was blind! ... They were all blind!

He had never come to hate his brother, not when he vilely murdered his father, as in those moments. An uncontrollable fury seized her with a force that completely dominated her.

"We must hurry, Karl! Those bandits must be passing through the gallery and will soon be breaking through to catch you off guard.

He stroked the hair of his "Nitchevo" with a tenderness that certainly expressed the violence of his love. But inside Karl's brain, ideas were coming together in a plan that would forever derail the sinister purposes of his enemy.

Forcing Irina to take a well-deserved rest, after exchanging her soaked clothes for those of a German soldier, the captain summoned his officers, informing them of the maneuver they had to perform.

A new atmosphere reigned inside the fort. The arrival of "Nitchevo" had been like a gigantic injection of optimism for Trauber's men. Furthermore, when the precious information that the young woman had brought was known in detail, the physical blackness of blindness, was crossed by a ray of luminous hope that powerfully lifted everyone's spirits.

They worked hard, not allowing themselves the slightest rest, while the noise of Semurow's men making their way into the cellars reached their ears.

* * *

"What's the matter, Kupriew?

They marched through the gallery, brightly lit by the lanterns of the advancing soldiers, their weapons at the ready.

Kupriew turned his face to his boss, who was walking beside him.

"What were you saying, Comrade Semurow?

Igor let out a short, cutting laugh.

"You are definitely over the moon, old friend! But, what you don't know is that your boss, Igor, reads in the eyes of his men like in an open book "then, with an urgent voice that did not allow any reply": You are going to tell me immediately what is wrong with you, Kupriew . Understood?

The Russian thought, at full speed, what he should do. If he lied to Igor, it was more than possible that Igor realized the deception and things would end badly right there. The best thing would be to tell the truth. After or during combat, a good opportunity may well be found to eliminate your boss without arousing the suspicions of others. In such a state of affairs, he would be the one to replace Igor.

"I have found Irina" he said without daring to look the other in the face.

Semurow's left hand closed around his arm with such force that Kupriew feared it would fracture it.

"Irina? You're lying, you filthy dog!

"I'm not lying, Igor. I recently found it next to the gallery.

The other released his arm.

"Can you tell me why you haven't taken her to camp? "And after a short pause" How you touched her, I'll make you burn alive!

"I have not done her any wrong," Kupriew hastened to say. I wanted him to speak to you quietly, before introducing himself to you. He's very afraid of you, Semurow.

He let out another of his usual sardonic giggles. Then, swiftly drawing the pistol, he unloaded the magazine on Kupriew.

"Did you want to keep it for yourself, old comrade? Is not that? You already knew, however, for a long time, since we lived in Tepluja, that Irina was not for you ... A blacksmith! The war has upset you, old comrade, and look where you have come by not knowing how to wait. A little more patience and you would have had as many beautiful women from Berlin you would have wanted ... But ... you were in a great hurry ... and you've always been like that, you old pig.

Once at the end of the gallery, Semurow's men quickly began their work. After clearing a large area of debris, they began to pick their way upward at peak force. Finally, when Igor realized how slowly the work was progressing, he promptly changed tactics.

"Lay down a load of TNT! We will break through immediately. Then we will enter the fort and kill them like rabbits.

What, indeed, could poor blind men do? They would receive the death blow, without realizing exactly where it was coming from. The battle, if it could be named, would be child's play for the men of Semurow.

The blast opened a hole large enough for four men to pass through at the same time. Before the smoke dissolved, Igor, holding the pistol, uttered a battle cry.

"Let's go guys! Hunt Nazis!

* * *

From the secluded mound on which Trauber's Company was situated, Irina Semurow, who had begged everyone to continue to call her "Nitchevo," gazed intently at the sinister silhouette of Lotzzy's fortress.

Karl had prepared everything for an exceptional reception to the partisans and together with the young woman, he hoped that her beautiful eyes, the only ones capable of piercing the darkness that had fallen on his, could warn him of the entry of his enemies.

His hands rested on the mechanical switch, whose cable snaked to the blockhouse. Everything was in that tremendous and empty tranquility that seems to announce great catastrophes.

A small explosion reached everyone's ears.

"They must have pierced the basement floor! Trauber warned.

Then he was silent. He guessed at his men, their faces stretched out towards the fort, eager for "Nitchevo" to give the order that everyone was waiting for.

After a while, in which everything was settled, the invaders' cries reached them. Irina, from her observation post, saw the reflection of the lanterns of Igor's men that had penetrated inside the fort.

One of those lights could be in his brother's hands. For a moment, her heart stopped the usual rhythm of its beats, as anguish washed over her. But almost immediately, the image of her father and Karl, their eyes dull in horrible darkness, brought blood to her cheeks again.

"Shoot, Trauber!

Karl flipped the switch, trying, his eyes blind and his face turned forward, to catch some of the flare from the explosion.

But the only person who had to squint was Irina ...

The tremendous lightning illuminated the region as in broad daylight. Then the explosion made heaven and earth tremble as if shaken by a painful shudder.

Slowly, the silence was killing the last echoes that rolled over the earth ...

At the head of the Company, which was moving away towards the West, Irina was on the arm of her beloved. All the sad memories of his life had been erased, definitively, with the explosion that seemed to have destroyed them forever.

From among the ranks, the first measure of "Marlene" began to be heard. Little by little, the clamor of the song grew until it occupied the entire scope of the universe that surrounded them.

The voices, sonorous, powerful and virile, were weaving, in the night air, "the one outside and the one that each one had in their eyes" the legend of an atrocious struggle that no generation could ever forget.

And, while the song resounded in her breasts, like a rhythm of hope that no defeat could quench, "Nitchevo" leaning on her lover, with her head on his chest and hearing the phrases of the melody from his lips,

ied and he laughed in a mixture of happiness and illusion, his gaze on
ie uncertain horizon where the sun had set.

END